SEQUENCES

SEQUENCES

By
SIEGFRIED SASSOON

NEW YORK
THE VIKING PRESS
1957

Published by the Viking Press
625 Madison Avenue, New York
March 1957
Printed in Great Britain

To
H. M. TOMLINSON

CONTENTS

COMMON CHORDS

RELEASE	page 3
THE UNPROVEN	4
EUPHRASY	5
AN EXAMPLE	6
AT MAX GATE	7
THE MESSAGE	8
AN ABSENTEE	9
THE HARDENED HEART	10
IN TIME OF DECIVILISATION	11
A 1940 MEMORY	12
A POST-MORTEM	13
ELSEWHERE	14
MAN AND DOG	15
CONTEMPORARY CHRISTMAS	16
PRAISE PERSISTENT	17
AN ASKING	18
RESURRECTION	19
REDEMPTION	20

EMBLEMS OF EXPERIENCE

A PRAYER TO TIME	*page* 23
TRAVELLING LIBRARY	24
WREN AND MAN	25
SOLITUDES AT SIXTY	26
ULTIMATE VALUES	27
OLD FASHIONED WEATHER	28
EARLY MARCH	29
ON SCRATCHBURY CAMP	30
A FALLODON MEMORY	31
A PROPRIETOR	32
CLEANING THE CANDELABRUM	33
AWARENESS OF ALCUIN	34
ASSOCIATES	35
A DREAM	36
ACCEPTANCE	37
BEFRIENDING STAR	38
THE NEED	39
WORLD WITHOUT END	40
THE MESSENGER	41
THE PRESENT WRITER	42

THE TASKING

THE TASKING	*page* 45
RETREAT FROM ETERNITY	46
THE VISITANT	47
THE QUESTION	48
THE MAKING	49
THE DISPERSAL	50
FAITH UNFAITHFUL	51
THE DARKNESS	52
THE CONTENTION	53
CAN IT BE?...	54
THE TRIAL	55
ANOTHER SPRING	56
THE HALF CENTURY	57
THE WELCOMING	58
THE WORST OF IT	59
THE BEST OF IT	60
THE ALLIANCE	61
HUMAN BONDAGE	62
AN EPITOME	63
RENEWALS	64
OCTOBER TREES	65
SIC SEDEBAT	66
THE HUMBLED HEART	67
A CHORD	68

COMMON CHORDS

Release

One winter's end I much bemused my head
In tasked attempts to drive it up to date
With what the undelighting moderns said
   Forecasting human fate.

And then, with nothing unforeseen to say
And no belief or unbelief to bring,
Came, in its old unintellectual way,
   The first real day of spring.

The Unproven

Looking at Life, some unbelieved-in angels
  Asked one another when
Science would overhear them and encourage
  Their ministries to men.

Listening outside Eternity for Knowledge
  And divination of Death
Stood Science. Hushed was Heaven; and all those angels,
  Still hopeful, held their breath.

Euphrasy

The large untidy February skies—
Some cheerful starlings screeling on a tree—
West wind and low-shot sunlight in my eyes—
    Is this decline for me?

The feel of winter finishing once more—
Sense of the present as a tale half told—
The land of life to look at and explore—
    Is this, then, to grow old?

An Example

I stood below a beech
And said to stillness, teach
Tranquillity. I told
Dumb patient earth to hold
My unquiet mind from speech.

A cole tit in the tree
Pecked, flitted, marked by me
Around whom nothing stirred
But this food-finding bird.

The moments passed; and I
No self-concernment knew
But one small purposed thing
Which from my presence flew
On deft unstartled wing...
And I was tranquil too.

At Max Gate

Old Mr Hardy, upright in his chair,
Courteous to visiting acquaintance chatted
With unaloof alertness while he patted
The sheep dog whose society he preferred.
He wore an air of never having heard
That there was much that needed putting right.
Hardy, the Wessex wizard, wasn't there.
Good care was taken to keep him out of sight.

Head propped on hand, he sat with me alone,
Silent, the log fire flickering on his face.
Here was the seer whose words the world had known.
Someone had taken Mr Hardy's place.

The Message

Toward sunset this November day, so stilled
And acquiescent in the year's decline,
I, riding slowly homeward, saw the sky
Transfigured as by beneficence fulfilled.
Thus Nature's countenance. The thought was merely
    mine.

Cloud streaks and shoals, like silver wings outspread,
Spanned innocent serenities of blue,
As though, enharmonised with life below,
Some heavenly minded message had been said.
Thus, childlike, I imagined. Yet it might be true.

An Absentee

Mercy. It seems a word
Seldom in these times heard.
Once urged on human hearts,
Its meaning, sweet to some,
Has for too many become
A presence that departs.

No nation, in its need,
Mercy's name must heed.
No statesman dare suggest
Methods by mercy bless'd.
   Most minds decide to-day
   That mercy does not pay.

The Hardened Heart

When things were in their pride,
And Youth with morning mind
Went lost and ardent eyed
Down by the broadening stream,
How could he·think to find
That life beloved had lied—
Its promise undesigned
Discordant to his dream?

While circumstance-led so,
How could he choose but go
To the music of delight?
Or how with laughter learn
On roads of no return
To numb his heart and know
The ugly facts of night?

In Time of Decivilisation

In August evening west
No sign of world unrest.
Goldening with gentle glow
The crowns of crowded trees,
Blue days decline and go
Bourdoned by bumble bees.

In twilight windowed room
Grave music of the mind
Companions me, for whom
Lost youth shouts far behind.
Not now life's overlord,
Only as viol to string
Vibrant, I would accord
With time's importuning.

Stillness, man's final friend,
Absolve this turmoiled thought
Of ills I cannot mend
That so my brain be brought
An unimpassioned pride
Where perfidies prevail,
And—old beliefs belied—
Philosophy to fail.

A 1940 Memory

One afternoon of war's worst troubles,
Disconsolate on autumn stubbles,
I marked what rarely rambles by—
A Clouded Yellow butterfly.

From those appalled and personal throes
Time will dissolve the pain, one knows;
And days when direful news was heard
Be indistinct, unreal, and blurred.

Yet, every walk I pass that way,
A sunless mid-September day
Will faithfully recur, and I
Stalk that slow loitering butterfly.

A Post-Mortem

Searching for souvenirs among some rubble,
A post-atomic-warfare man observed
That 'those who made this little bit of trouble
Got only what they asked for and deserved'.
   Then, in a kindlier afterthought's release,
   He pitied 'them that only asked for peace'.

Elsewhere

Let Congresses consider how to avoid
These bomb abominations being employed
In suicidal conflict—how
To unannihilate the future now.

Since nothing that one man can think or say
Could prove effective in the feeblest way,
He, for appeasement of his tortured mind,
Must look elsewhere to be
Defended and befriended and resigned
And fortified and free.

Elsewhere. The indestructible exists
Beyond found formulas of scientists.
Our spiritual situation stood the same
In other epochs when
To thwart all ministries of mercy came
The arrogant inventiveness of men.

Man and Dog

Who's this—alone with stone and sky?
It's only my old dog and I—
It's only him; it's only me;
Alone with stone and grass and tree.

What share we most—we two together?
Smells, and awareness of the weather.
What is it makes us more than dust?
My trust in him; in me his trust.

Here's anyhow one decent thing
That life to man and dog can bring;
One decent thing, remultiplied
Till earth's last dog and man have died.

Contemporary Christmas

Bells, that on this immaculate morn
Rung in redeeming Christ reborn,
What tidings brought you then?
We did our best, the bells reply,
To broadcast, as in years gone by,
Peace and good-will to men.

Priest, on whose lips the evangel rings
Of Mercy from the King of Kings
For creatures error imbued,
Perhaps you felt, this fated year,
The Virgin Birth a not so clear
Evidence of hope renewed?

No answer comes. No answer can
Contain—this Christmastide of Man—
The world's predicament.
Meanwhile I deem, as well one might,
That phantom powers around us fight
An Armageddon of Dark and Light
Whereof we wait the event.

Praise Persistent

Alone with life, I heard massed choirs declare
For humankind conjunction with the unseen
Essence which rules redemption. On the air
Hosanna in excelsis swelled serene
As through cathedral'd centuries that have been.

This was the moment's affirmation. And then
On gloom-girt winds of time I heard it blown
With dwindling resonance, from mouths of men
Forever claiming kinship with the unknown—
Forever their one hope on earth pursuing
In perishable pilgrimage, in doomed defeat,
Fooled by phantasms that wreak their dire undoing,
Yet mindful of the Maker they would meet.

Thus, praise persistent, year beyond wrought year,
Those paeans rise and fade and disappear—
Held to what infinite heart—heard by what immanent ear?

An Asking

Primordial Cause, your creature questions why
Law has empowered him with this central I;
Asks how to carnal consciousness you brought
Spirit, the unexplained of sovereign thought;
And whence your influent essence quickened first
In hungry heart, and brain's unscienced thirst.
My heritage I ponder. Who was he,
In geologic gloomed pre-history,
That glimpsed beyond his death-environed cave
The soul—a star—a gift he yet might save?

Resurrection

Suppose, some quiet afternoon in spring,
The hour of judgement came
For me and my mistakes when journeying
Along with that defence for nullity, my name.
Suppose, while sauntering in the primrosed wood,
To body and soul's dispute a voice cried *halt*,
And I that instant stood
Absolved of unfulfilment and essential fault.

Suppose this resurrection, this release,
This self-surrender wrought;
And the word heard within, *Depart in peace*;
Take to the everlasting all that time has taught...
What, for the spiritual service some foresee
Beyond probational breath,
Would then emerge from marred and mystic me
To stand with those white presences delivered
    through death?

Redemption

I thought; These multitudes we hold in mind—
This host of souls redeemed—
Out of the abysm of the ages came—
Out of the spirit of man—devised or dreamed.

I thought; To the Invisible I am blind;
No angels tread my nights with feet of flame;
No mystery is mine—
No whisper from that world beyond my sense.

I think; If through some chink in me could shine
But once—O but one ray
From that all-hallowing and eternal day,
Asking no more of Heaven I would go hence.

EMBLEMS OF EXPERIENCE

A Prayer to Time

Time, that anticipates eternities
And has an art to resurrect the rose;
Time, whose lost siren song at evening blows
With sun-flushed cloud shoreward on toppling seas;
Time, arched by planets lonely in the vast
Sadness that darkens with the fall of day;
Time, unexplored elysium; and the grey
Death-shadow'd pyramid that we name the past—
   Magnanimous Time, patient with man's vain glory;
   Ambition's road; Lethe's awaited guest;
   Time, hearkener to the stumbling passionate story
   Of human failure humanly confessed;
   Time, on whose stair we dream our hopes of heaven,
   Help us to judge ourselves, and so be shriven.

Travelling Library

Signing a letter with my monogram—
To someone more than fifty years beknown—
I thought, computing worldwork self's been shown,
What an old library of life I am!

What self's been shown? What self had learnt from selves
While multiple they merged, each into each;
This, for the central student they could teach,
Remains most valued volume on my shelves.

Wren and Man

What does it mean to call oneself a man,
As though to no one else the name applied?
I tried to think. Before my thoughts began
Some voice quite unexpectedly replied—
    'This afternoon, as you remember, came
    And flew around your room a Jennie Wren...
    Not till that nimble creature knows its name
    Will you have learnt your meaning among men.'

Solitudes at Sixty

Sexagenarian solitudes, I find,
Are somewhat stagnant, motiveless and slow:
Old friends arrive; but only to my mind,
Since their earth-farings ended years ago.
Beloved or valued ghosts, these reappear
At my peculiar prompting. Known by heart,
Finite impersonations, learnt by ear,
Their voices talk in character and depart.

They, once my wise and faithful, have no being:
No supersensual agency can bring
Those presences from silence and unseeing:
They dwell secure from world's importuning.
Meanwhile myself sits with myself agreeing
That to be sixty is no easy thing.

Ultimate Values

The hour grows late, and I outlive my friends,
Remaining, since I must, with memoried mind
That for consolement deepeningly depends
On hoarded time, enriched and redesigned.
So is it with us all. And thus we find
Endeared survivals that our thought defends.

What now, from eyed experience, haunts my ears,
Endenizened within me, heart and head?
Mostly those things which touched the source of tears,
Those word-illumined moments, seen and said,
Those wisdoms, mortalised beyond the years
By simplest human utterance of the dead.

Old Fashioned Weather

This New Year's nightfall, clinching grasp of cold
Began to blur my warm room's window panes,
Iced over soon with traceries formed like fronds.
Hard weather, sexton's ally for the old,
Nevertheless jogs memory that regains
The glow and glee of boyhood skating ponds.

Indulgent of that obvious thought, I've tried
Conclusions with another, also trite,
Yet welcome, in an age of values lost.
Traditions perish; topsy-turvyfied,
Our once well-wonted usages take flight;
But not so when we get a spell of frost.

Weather's the same for all. Though Science tells
The world to-day what Newton never guessed,
He woke to sunshine sparkling on crisp snow;
Heard, clear across white pastures, midnight bells,
And thought, as I do now, with quiet zest,
Of New Year's Eve a century ago.

Early March

March having come this year mild, hazy-skied and calm,
With hill-top airs from northward breathing frost-like smell,
I dawdle along the lane that leads to Sundial Farm.

Beguilements (which my middle-age can't yet dispel)
Steal into me. Rejuvenescence works its charm.
Designlessly in love with life unlived, I go
Content with the mere fact that fields are drying fast
And tiny beads of bud along the hedge foreshow
The blackthorn winter that will come too late to last.

Beyond that bare untidy orchard, now and then,
One thrush half tells how in the twilight hour he'll sing
To no one but himself his wild belief in spring.
Meanwhile I'm thankful for this almost dusty road,
Celandine's lowly gold, and daylight lengthening when
The winterbournes, like time, past February have flowed.

On Scratchbury Camp

Along the grave green downs, this idle afternoon,
Shadows of loitering silver clouds, becalmed in blue,
Bring, like unfoldment of a flower, the best of June.

Shadows outspread in spacious movement, always you
Have dappled the downs and valleys at this time of year,
While larks, ascending shrill, praised freedom as they flew.

Now, through that song, a fighter-squadron's drone I hear
From Scratchbury Camp, whose turfed and cowslip'd rampart seems
More hill than history, ageless and oblivion-blurred.

I walk the fosse, once manned by bronze and flint-head spear:
On war's imperious wing the shafted sun-ray gleams:
One with the warm sweet air of summer stoops the bird.

Cloud shadows, drifting slow like heedless daylight dreams,
Dwell and dissolve; uncircumstanced they pause and pass.
I watch them go. My horse, contented, crops the grass.

A Fallodon Memory

One afternoon I watched him as he stood
In the twilight of his wood.
Among the firs he'd planted, forty years away,
Tall, and quite still, and almost blind,
World patience in his face, stood Edward Grey;
Not listening,
For it was at the end of summer, when no birds sing:
Only the bough's faint dirge accompanied his mind
Absorbed in some Wordsworthian slow self-communing.

In lichen-coloured homespun clothes he seemed
So merged with stem and branch and twinkling leaves
That almost I expected, looking away, to find
When glancing there again, that I had daylight dreamed
His figure, as when some trick of sun and shadow deceives.

But there he was, haunting heart-known ancestral ground;
Near to all Nature; and in that nearness somehow strange;
Whose native humour, human-simple yet profound,
And strength of spirit no calamity could change.
To whom, designed for countrified contentments, came
Honours unsought and unrewarding foreign fame:
And, at the last, that darkened world wherein he moved
In memoried deprivation of life once learnt and loved.

A Proprietor

A meditative man
Walks in this wood, and calls each tree his own:
Yet the green track he treads is older than
Recorded English history:
His feet, while moving on toward times unknown,
Travel from traceless mystery.
Wondering what manner of men
Will walk there in the problem'd future when
Those trees he planted are long fallen or felled,
He twirls a white wild violet in his fingers
As others may when he's no more beheld,
Nor memory of him lingers.

Cleaning the Candelabrum

While cleaning my old six-branched candelabrum
(Which disconnects in four and twenty parts)
I think how other hands its brass have brightened,
And wonder what was happening in their hearts:
I wonder what they mused about—those ghosts—
In what habitual prosy-morning'd places,
Who furbished these reflections, humming softly
With unperplexed or trouble-trodden faces.

While rubbing up the ring by which one lifts it,
I visualise some Queen Anne country squire
Guiding a guest from dining-room to parlour
Where port and filberts wait them by the fire:
Or—in the later cosmos of Miss Austen—
Two spinsters, wavering shadows on a wall,
Conferring volubly about Napoleon
And what was worn at the Assembly Ball.

Then, thought-reverting to the man who made it
With long-apprenticed unpresuming skill,
When earth was yet unwarned of Electricity
And rush-lights gave essential service still,
I meditate upon mankind's advancement
From flint sparks into million-volted glare
That shows us everything except the future—
And leaves us not much wiser than we were.

Dim lights have had their day; wax candles even
Produce a conscious 'period atmosphere'.
But brass out-twinkles time; my candelabrum
Persists well on toward its three hundredth year,
And has illuminated, one might say,
Much vista'd history, many vanished lives...
Meanwhile for me, outside my open window,
The twilight blackbird flutes, and spring arrives.

Awareness of Alcuin

At peace in my tall-windowed Wiltshire room,
(Birds overheard from chill March twilight's close)
I read, translated, Alcuin's verse, in whom
A springtide of resurgent learning rose.

Homely and human, numb in feet and fingers,
Alcuin believed in angels; asked their aid;
And still the essence of that asking lingers
In the aureoled invocation which he made
For Charlemagne, his scholar. Alcuin, old,
Loved listening to the nest-near nightingale,
Forgetful of renown that must enfold
His world-known name; remembering pomps that fail.

Alcuin, from temporalities at rest,
Sought grace within him, given from afar;
Noting how sunsets worked around to west;
Watching, at spring's approach, that beckoning star;
And hearing, while one thrush sang through the rain,
Youth, which his soul in Paradise might regain.

Associates

It was not thus while we were young—
Not thus for us
When breath was bold and heart hope toward
The future flung,
And hours could shine like towers where bells
Are wildly rung.

It was not so for you and me—
Not so, we know,
When body and being owned the earth
And each was free.
A way-worn man within you dwells,
And I am he.

A Dream

I met a stranger on the brink of sleep:
Hooded he stood, whose eyes acknowledged sorrow.
He wrote across the darkness of my mind
One word, *Tomorrow*.

Through dream we went. Our way was cragged and steep,
And what the future told we might not find.
Then in that face which I had thought unknown
I recognised my own.

'Stranger,' I said, 'since you and I are one,
'Let us go back. Let us undo what's done.'

Acceptance

Man, who by youth beguiled has trusted time and thriven—
Man, from whose tortured lips the lie to life was given—
Man, dumbly reconciled to suffer where he had striven—
  Simpleton, accuser, and acceptor, each in turn
  Mortality's enigma must enact and learn,
   Till, in the presence of his one deliverer, death,
   'Take not Thy holy Spirit from us, Lord,' Man saith.

Befriending Star

Befriending star, low hung above the mountain gloom,
Empower my human frailty to conceive you kind:
Be only what these earth-homed eyes behold, for whom
Aeonian-rapt remoteness overwhelms the mind.

Withdraw, while watched by me, your magnitude—your dire
Unmeaningness for man. Heart-simplified, appear
Not in ferocity of elemental fire,
But, for my lowly faith, a sign by which to steer.

The Need

Nobody knows
Whither our delirium of invention goes,
Who turn toward time to come
Alone with heart-beats, marching to that muffled drum.
Nobody hears
Bells from beyond the silence of the years
That wait for those unborn.
O God within me, speak from your mysterious morn.

Speak, through the few,
Your light of life to nourish us anew.
Speak, for our world possessed
By demon influences of evil and unrest.
Act, as of old,
That we some dawnlit destiny may behold
From this doom-darkened place.
O move in mercy among us. Grant accepted grace.

World Without End

First-found beliefs remain. I cannot free
My thought from looking on Eternity
As highway for the unresting soul of Man.
For though there be no everlasting life in me,
No end I see to what the idea of God began.

Innocent conceptions change. No more I find
Notioned Eternity in telescopes
Exploring timeless time. Yet, in my mind,
It dwells as when for childhood fatherly designed
To be enduring home for heart-envisioned hopes.

I see my self, one body on that invisible road;
Brief bird on air, blind burrowing mole, dumb fish in stream.
I trust Eternity as being's elect abode,
Where the idea of God pervades our daunted dream.

The Messenger

Mind, busy in the body's life-lit room;
Seldom in strength, unpiloted at best;
How ignorant you admit from outer gloom
The soul, in all God's world, most welcome guest.

These two, it seems, are separate. The soul
On incorporeal errands comes and goes
With rumours and reportings from the Whole
For mind, which only brain experience knows.

Poor mortal mind, when you, in me, decay—
When once delighting faculties grow dim—
Cry on the parting soul for power to say,
With passion, 'I befriended was by Him.'

The Present Writer

An evening lamp; and something shown
From archives of experience known.
A fire-conditioned solitude
By outlived ardencies imbued.

A memoried mind afoot to find
Rewards from failure left behind,
And by matured awareness told
How much of life the heart can hold—
How little, in life employed and planned,
The gnomic head may understand.

Thought-haunted room; and one for whom
Departure and disfleshment loom.
The ticking clock at evening's end;
And sleep,—thwart self's enfolding friend.

THE TASKING

The Tasking

To find rewards of mind with inward ear
Through silent hours of seeking;
To put world sounds behind and hope to hear
Instructed spirit speaking:

Sometimes to catch a clue from selfhood's essence
And ever that revealment to be asking;
This—and through darkness to divine God's presence—
I take to be my tasking.

Retreat from Eternity

Just now I stared out on a star-strange night
With man's habitual wonder at the sight,
And the old lonely question—stellar space
Coincident wherefore with one human face?

Then, while the firelight flickered, musing here,
I saw, in mimic constellation shown,
Reflected sparkles on the chandelier,
And was no more benumbed by the unknown.

The Visitant

Someone else I know of—neither young nor old—
Seated late at night in my accustomed chair,
Willed to an intended thing which must be told,
Catches intimations brought from otherwhere.

Someone else invades me for an hour or two.
Clocked occluded self wrote never lines like his.
Me he has no need of. And I know not who
Or from what irrational inwardness he is.

The Question

What am I then? A consciousness that cries
Good morning and good night;
A brevity whose eyes look once on light:
One thought in all the unmindful mind of nature;
One face in multitudes a moment seen;
Eternity's quick creature, born of what has been.

The Making

This making is a mystery. Me He made
And left to build my being as best I could:
A child afraid who for protection prayed,
Worsted by wrong, but wanting to grow good
A man betrayed yet blessed by circumstance,
Seeking self-knowledge, learning through mistake,
To shaped experience half compelled by chance.
What work was His, where mind its self must make?

*It is He that hath made us, and not we
Ourselves.* One moment's aftercome I live,
Flawed with inherited humanity,
And fooled by imperfections wrought through race.
This He first fashioned; this He can forgive
When granting His unapprehended grace.

The Dispersal

Speaking as one world to another,
From finite toward the fabulous, I
Question my condition in survival,
Should such be destined when we die.

If Nature be indeed our mother,
(Neglectful parent though she seem)
What must remain on my arrival
From earth's anthropocentric dream?

How do you handle my dispersal—
Nameless, unlanguaged, and deminded?
Shall psyche thrive, no more purblinded?
Answer me that, O Universal.

Faith Unfaithful

Mute, with signs I speak:
Blind, by groping seek:
Heed; yet nothing hear:
Feel; find no one near.

Deaf, eclipsed, and dumb,
Through this gloom I come
On the time-path trod
Toward ungranted God.

Carnal, I can claim
Only His known name.
Dying, can but be
One with Him in me.

The Darkness

The room, the darkness, and the bed;
Quick ticks the clock; sleep comes not nigh:
A melancholy mind must lie
With troublings of its wakeful head.

Winter without. Assurance spent.
A stormy surge of woods around
My house where, blending in the sound,
I think how on the winds life went.

Heard now, but inly taken breath;
Known, but the animate self alone:
And sleep's approaching presence shown
In semblance of undreaming death.

The Contention

Then came a cry, 'No spirit—none—
'Within your deathward being dwells:
'The will of darkness must be done:
'Take this, and make the most of what your timepiece tells.'

I knew, unknowing; I heard, unhearing,
A voice beyond my bodily boding,
'The faithful found me without fearing:
'Learn this, and look forever toward your soul's unloading.'

Can it be?...

Can it be, that beyond and above human behaviour
Measureless mercy and love, sought for as saviour,
Fold every mortal who kneels frustrate with living,
Lift by the light that reveals faith and forgiving?

Can it be, that masterful mind, shrewd in its season,
Resolute only to find rightness through reason,
Bold in the doubt which denies world beyond seeing,
Dooms to deception the wise blest in their being?

The Trial

Unscientific selfhood, often drawn
To dwell with mystical imaginings,
Zealous to walk the way of Henry Vaughan
Who glimpsed divinity in speechless things,
How fare you on that faithful pilgrimage,
Environed by an unbelieving age?

Ask the night sky for intimations of God.
Moves mercy there? Astronomy replies
With numbers of light-years each twinkle has trod.
Question the tropical jungle, through what guise
He manifests therein His ministrant law,
And how he justifies fang, swamp, and claw.

Nature and knowledge daunt with dire denial
The inward witness and the innocent dream.
On such rough road must faith endure its trial,
Upheld by resolution to redeem
The soul, that world within an ignorant shape
One with the solar system and the ape.

Another Spring

Aged self, disposed to lose his hold on life,
Looks down, at winter's ending, and perceives
Continuance in some crinkled primrose leaves.

A noise of nesting rooks in tangled trees.
Stillness—inbreathed, expectant. Shadows that bring
Cloud-castled thoughts from downland distances.
Eyes, ears are old. But not the sense of spring.

Look, listen, live, some inward watcher warns.
Absorb this moment's meaning: and be wise
With hearts whom the first primrose purifies.

The Half Century

A boyhood, ardent minded to achieve
Its vision of the ideal in vigilant verse.
An old man, blindly asking to believe
World wickedness foredoomed to work no worse.

Youth, following fantasies he took for truth,
Led by his heart's hosannas overheard.
Age, reading in the book of life with ruth
For innocents who wait the unwritten word.

The Welcoming

Lovely for youth, the look on life's lit face,
And limitless his longing
All beckonings and beguilements to embrace.
Unseen, those spectres thronging.

Marvel, the mind's emergence innocent-eyed,
Unblemished and believing.
World welcomed he, who goes without a guide
Toward wrongs beyond retrieving.

The Worst of It

Here's Man, with all that knowledge to his name,
All that magnificent music in his mind,
And long achieved reliance on the soul.

Here's Man, empowered by armaments of flame,
Unfuturing his future; self-assigned
To suicide, through the secrets which he stole.

Here's Me; who neither ask nor aim to be
More than the mote in heaven's realéd ray.
Here's Life, that might move fortunate and free,
Condemned by circumstance to doom's dismay.

The Best of It

Spring, surgent in the sense-delighted blood;
In daybreak being all the burst of bud.
This, beyond argument, was well begun.

Prosperities of summer that pervade
Ongoing while headstrong hope and vision are made
Aware and eager. Nothing there to shun.

Autumnal toned attainment, trouble-taught
To mastery of emotion-hindered thought.
Passion outlived. Regret there need be none.

Star-sown eternity for mindsight old.
Winter endured. Time past a tale retold.
Wisdom and wonder, faithful to enfold
Life, that by no disaster is undone.

The Alliance

'You figure of flesh, abode of appetites,
'Duped by mean motives, frivolous in feeling,
'Go your own gait; enjoy those gross delights.
'I work elsewhere, in search of heaven-sent healing.'

Thus bragged the spirit, positive in pride,
Till from far off a wisening voice replied—
'Of body and soul there can be no division;
'Soul should embrace it, cherish and control.
'Our two great halves must share a single vision.
'Let mutual services unite them whole.'

Then spirit asked forgiveness of the brain;
And all went well. The speaker was Montaigne.

Human Bondage

I know a night of stars within me;
Through eyes of dream I have perceived
Blest apparitions who would win me
Home to what innocence believed.

I know a universe beyond me;
Power that pervades the fluctuant soul,
Signalling my brain it would unbond me
And make heart's imperfection whole.

I, the chance-comer from creation,
Blind subject to defending day;
I, this blithe structure of sensation,
Prisoned and impassioned by my clay.

An Epitome

Just thinking...Yet it may be that
My thought, which for a moment held
What seemed mind-life's epitome
From infanthood to eld,
Spoke the one word in all my time
To make endured existence known
Even as it is. *Accept your soul.*
Be evermore alone.

Renewals

I said to downcast eyes—
Look up; accept surprise
Which waits, all welcomings.
I said to shuttered ears—
Heed how earth music nears
On wonder's wind-swept strings.

Unquesting heart I told
To be made manifold
Through love's resurgent will.
I said to fitful mind—
Put discontents behind;
Be silent and grow still.

October Trees

How innocent were these
Trees, that in mist-green May,
Blown by a prospering breeze,
Stood garlanded and gay;
Who now in sundown glow
Of serious colour clad
Confront me with their show
As though resigned and sad.

Trees who unwhispering stand
Umber and bronze and gold,
Pavilioning the land
For one grown tired and old;
Elm, chestnut, beech, and lime,
I am merged in you, who tell
Once more in tones of time
Your foliaged farewell.

Sic Sedebat

Little enough you've learnt
While being within you burnt,
Consuming nights and days
In brief oblivioned blaze:
Soon whisperless are we,
Said the fire to me.

Nothing tonight you know
How worldhood's workings go;
Of what the years have wrought
You hold no smouldering thought;
Toward kindled flames to come
Your divination is dumb:
Little the mind remembers,
Sighed the shifting embers.

The Humbled Heart

Go your seeking, soul.
Mine the proven path of time's foretelling.
Yours accordance with some mysteried whole.
I am but your passion-haunted dwelling.

Bring what news you can,
Stranger, loved of body's humbled heart.
Say one whispered word to mortal man
From that peace whereof he claims you part.

Hither-hence, my guest,
Blood and bone befriend, where you abide
Till withdrawn to share some timeless quest.
I am but the brain that dreamed and died.

A Chord

On stillness came a chord,
While I, the instrument,
Knew long-withheld reward:
Gradual the glory went;
Vibrating, on and on,
Toward harmony unheard,
Till dark where sanctus shone;
Lost, once a living word.

But in me yet abode
The given grace though gone;
The love, the lifted load,
The answered orison.